Written and Illustrated
by Caroll Simpson

WHALE
Child

HERITAGE

VICTORIA | VANCOUVER | CALGARY

One day, while flying over the Pacific Northwest coast, Eagle saw a village with a group of children playing on a boardwalk. He wondered if they knew what was coming.

With a big strong voice, a young boy stepped forward and proclaimed, "I am from the Eagle Clan!" A little girl turned to an older girl and asked, "Who are we, Big Sister?" "This is for us to find out!" Big Sister replied.

Eagle tried to warn the village, but no one listened. And then it happened. Volcano woke up from its long rest. "What is this horrendous noise?" the little girl cried. In her most protective voice, Big Sister said, "Do not worry. I will take care of you."

Mother Earth began to shake and rumble. The people grabbing their children and running to safety did not see the small girl, but Big Sister did. "Run to the canoe! Run!" cried Big Sister. The little girl ran down the beach and jumped into an empty canoe.

The canoe shook free and slid off the shore and out to sea, leaving the paddle behind. Over the monstrous noise of Volcano, Big Sister heard the little girl holler, "I will come back to find you!" Lost in all the noise, Big Sister's voice could not be heard to say,

"I will be here."

The canoe found itself in a swift southern current. Without a paddle, the girl was helpless. For many days, she asked every creature she saw, "Do you know where I am?" But no one replied. She saw Owl and asked, "Owl, do you know how I can get home?" But Owl said nothing.

Led down the coast by this strong river in the sea, the girl was caught in a violent storm. The wind and current threw the canoe about. **Killer Whale**, looking for a meal, saw the canoe in distress.

Grey Whale saw what was about to happen and smacked Killer Whale with her giant tail. Using her huge body, she blocked the violent waves from capsizing the canoe.

"Thank you, Mother Whale," the girl gasped.

The next morning, the land had changed. The young girl looked around for Mother Whale, wanting to ask where she was, but the whale was gone. Nothing looked the same. The seas had become glassy and strangely warm. "I am lost," whispered the girl.

The days that followed were long and hot. The rainwater that had collected in the canoe during the storm was nearly gone. The poor girl had not eaten for days. The sea was teeming with life, but there was no food for her. **"I am hungry,"** called the girl to the sea birds. "Will you please share your food?" They ignored her.

Never had the girl seen such unusual creatures. She wondered if they were real or if the Mother of the Ocean had sent visions to confuse her. Looking over the side of the canoe, the girl saw a giant spotted fish. "Can you tell me where I am?" she asked. But **Whale Shark** gave no reply.

There was no visit from the mist and rain of her lost world. No familiar animals came to help her. Many days passed, and the girl grew weak. "Mother Whale, where are you?" she called out in a small, trembling voice. **"Help me**, Mother Whale."

Mother Whale, who had been guiding the canoe the whole way, finally reached her destination—a warm, quiet bay guarded by giant cacti. Mother Whale wanted to help the girl, but she had something to do that could not be postponed.

"Hold on, little spirit," Mother Whale sang.

The bay was filled with mother, sister, aunt, and grandmother grey whales. They had all gathered to give birth or greet the new generation. The water reverberated with the magic of new life and songs of joy.

"**Welcome,** my daughter," Mother Whale sang to her newborn.

Mother Whale was happy. She knew this child was special.

"It is time to greet your **sister spirit,**" she sang as she pushed the baby whale upward.

Breaking the smooth surface of the water and taking her first breath, the baby whale drew in the spirit of the little girl in the lost canoe.

Filled with the human spirit, the baby whale felt strong, happy, and determined. **Whale Child**—the spirit of the girl united with the baby whale—was filled with questions. She did not know which to ask first. "Why are you white when all other whales are grey?" she asked her new sister spirit. Leaping with joy, the baby white whale replied, "Because you make me **special.**"

"Where am I going? Are we lost?" asked Whale Child.

"You are not lost," said White Whale.

"You are with me, and we are going north."

Travelling up the North American coast, the shoreline began to change. Whale Child asked, "Where in this big world is my village?" **"It is not far now,"** said White Whale. They travelled north for many days, and Whale Child searched the shoreline for her village.

The water got colder, and the fish began to look familiar. Giant evergreen trees stood tall along the rocky coast. Coming around a point and looking through the mist, Whale Child cried out, "Look! Look! There is my village!" As they swam closer to shore, she shouted, **"There is Big Sister!"**

With an empty but happy heart, White Whale swam close to the beach and released Whale Child into the surf. Splashing through the water towards her, Big Sister declared, "I will always take care of you!" "Yes," said Whale Child. "And the **Spirit of the Whale** will take care of us."

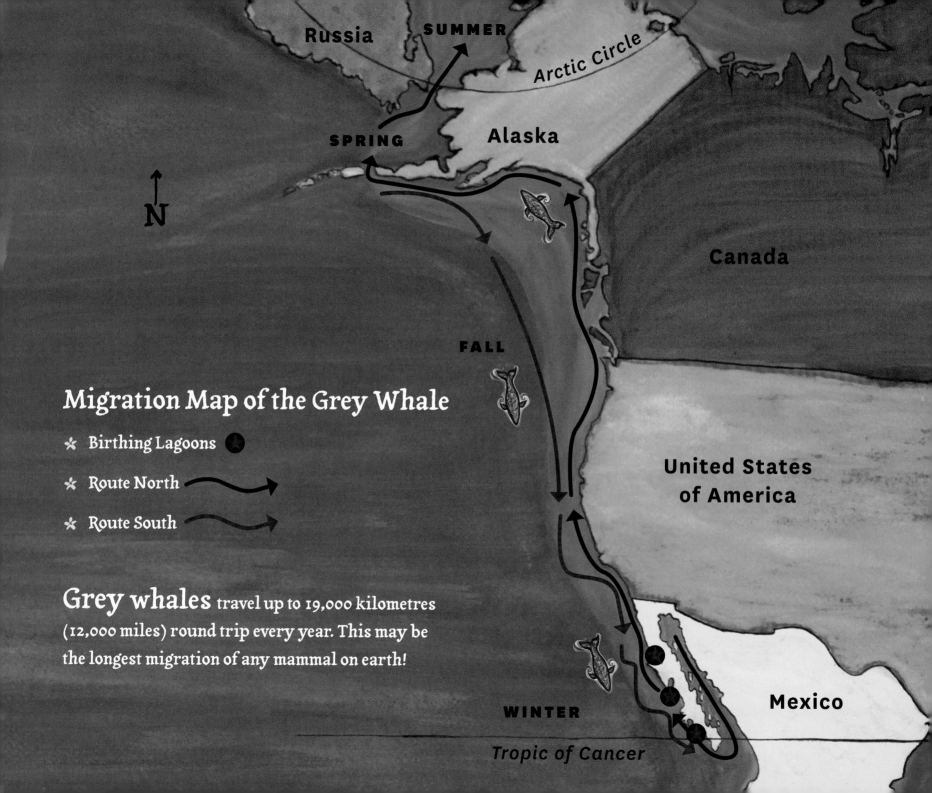

Russia

SUMMER

Arctic Circle

SPRING

Alaska

N

Canada

FALL

Migration Map of the Grey Whale

* Birthing Lagoons ●
* Route North →
* Route South →

United States
of America

Grey whales travel up to 19,000 kilometres (12,000 miles) round trip every year. This may be the longest migration of any mammal on earth!

WINTER

Mexico

Tropic of Cancer

SPRING MIGRATION: **January to June,** *Northbound*

Adult male, newly pregnant female, and juvenile grey whales are the first to head north. Mothers and calves stay several weeks longer preparing for this long journey. Using this extra time to feed on the rich milk of their mothers, the calves become stronger and put on a heavier layer of blubber. This will insulate them from the cold northern waters.

SUMMER FEEDING GROUNDS: **May to October**

When the ice melts in the Bering, Chukchi, and Beaufort Seas, Pacific grey whales start feeding on the tons of abundant food available. They gain hundreds of pounds of blubber. The whales use this stored energy for the annual trip to the lagoons in Mexico and back.

FALL MIGRATION: **October to February,** *Southbound*

The first to migrate south are pregnant females. They are in a hurry to arrive at Mexico's warm nursery lagoons. Right behind them are the males and other adult females. The youngsters join the journey south, but not all reach Mexico before they turn around and head north.

WINTER BIRTHING AND MATING GROUNDS: **December to April**

The lagoons of the Baja Peninsula in Mexico are perfect nurseries for newborn grey whales during their first few months of life. The mother's normal internal body temperature is about 38 degrees Celsius (99 degrees Fahrenheit). The newborns feel comfortable in the warm, shallow lagoons.

Northern Elements

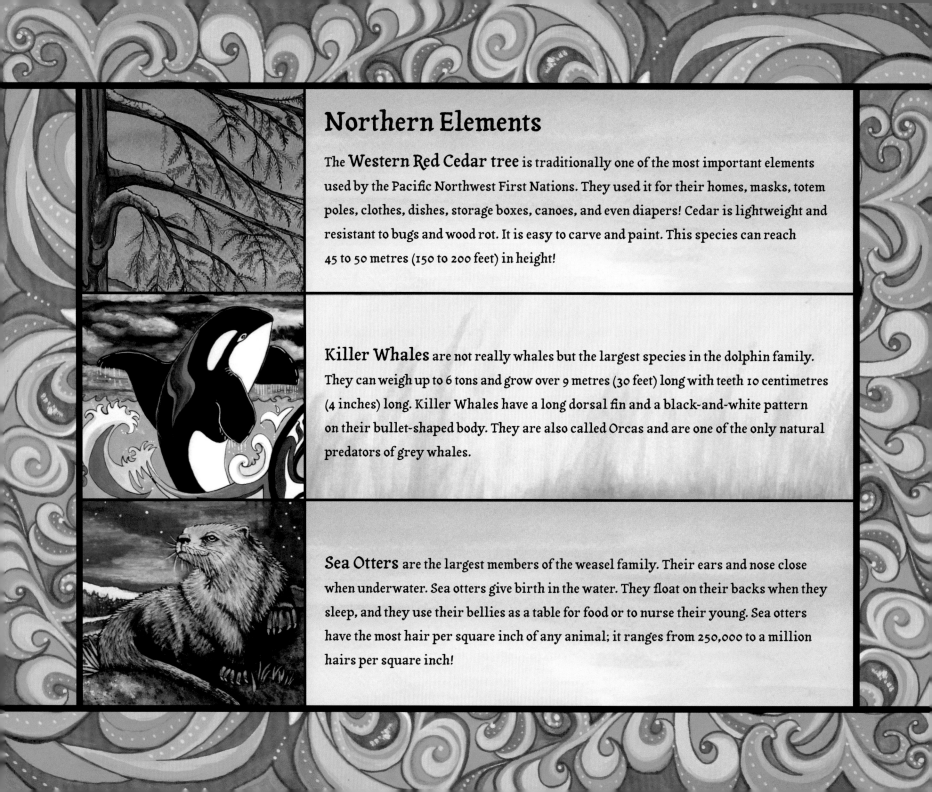

The **Western Red Cedar tree** is traditionally one of the most important elements used by the Pacific Northwest First Nations. They used it for their homes, masks, totem poles, clothes, dishes, storage boxes, canoes, and even diapers! Cedar is lightweight and resistant to bugs and wood rot. It is easy to carve and paint. This species can reach 45 to 50 metres (150 to 200 feet) in height!

Killer Whales are not really whales but the largest species in the dolphin family. They can weigh up to 6 tons and grow over 9 metres (30 feet) long with teeth 10 centimetres (4 inches) long. Killer Whales have a long dorsal fin and a black-and-white pattern on their bullet-shaped body. They are also called Orcas and are one of the only natural predators of grey whales.

Sea Otters are the largest members of the weasel family. Their ears and nose close when underwater. Sea otters give birth in the water. They float on their backs when they sleep, and they use their bellies as a table for food or to nurse their young. Sea otters have the most hair per square inch of any animal; it ranges from 250,000 to a million hairs per square inch!

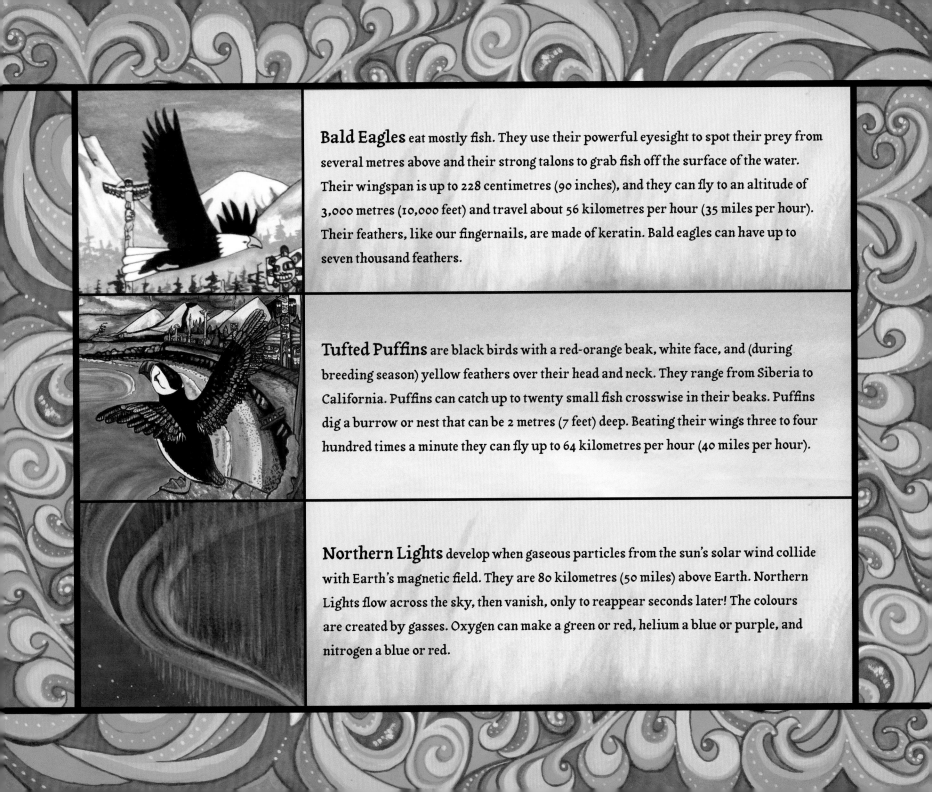

Bald Eagles eat mostly fish. They use their powerful eyesight to spot their prey from several metres above and their strong talons to grab fish off the surface of the water. Their wingspan is up to 228 centimetres (90 inches), and they can fly to an altitude of 3,000 metres (10,000 feet) and travel about 56 kilometres per hour (35 miles per hour). Their feathers, like our fingernails, are made of keratin. Bald eagles can have up to seven thousand feathers.

Tufted Puffins are black birds with a red-orange beak, white face, and (during breeding season) yellow feathers over their head and neck. They range from Siberia to California. Puffins can catch up to twenty small fish crosswise in their beaks. Puffins dig a burrow or nest that can be 2 metres (7 feet) deep. Beating their wings three to four hundred times a minute they can fly up to 64 kilometres per hour (40 miles per hour).

Northern Lights develop when gaseous particles from the sun's solar wind collide with Earth's magnetic field. They are 80 kilometres (50 miles) above Earth. Northern Lights flow across the sky, then vanish, only to reappear seconds later! The colours are created by gasses. Oxygen can make a green or red, helium a blue or purple, and nitrogen a blue or red.

Southern Elements

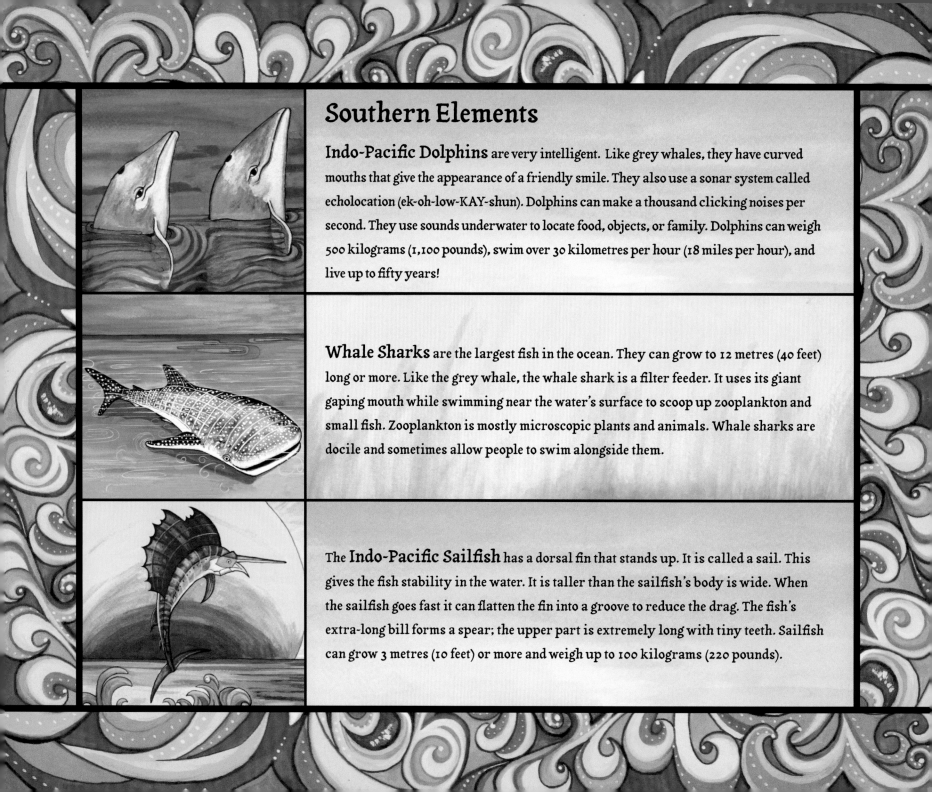

Indo-Pacific Dolphins are very intelligent. Like grey whales, they have curved mouths that give the appearance of a friendly smile. They also use a sonar system called echolocation (ek-oh-low-KAY-shun). Dolphins can make a thousand clicking noises per second. They use sounds underwater to locate food, objects, or family. Dolphins can weigh 500 kilograms (1,100 pounds), swim over 30 kilometres per hour (18 miles per hour), and live up to fifty years!

Whale Sharks are the largest fish in the ocean. They can grow to 12 metres (40 feet) long or more. Like the grey whale, the whale shark is a filter feeder. It uses its giant gaping mouth while swimming near the water's surface to scoop up zooplankton and small fish. Zooplankton is mostly microscopic plants and animals. Whale sharks are docile and sometimes allow people to swim alongside them.

The **Indo-Pacific Sailfish** has a dorsal fin that stands up. It is called a sail. This gives the fish stability in the water. It is taller than the sailfish's body is wide. When the sailfish goes fast it can flatten the fin into a groove to reduce the drag. The fish's extra-long bill forms a spear; the upper part is extremely long with tiny teeth. Sailfish can grow 3 metres (10 feet) or more and weigh up to 100 kilograms (220 pounds).

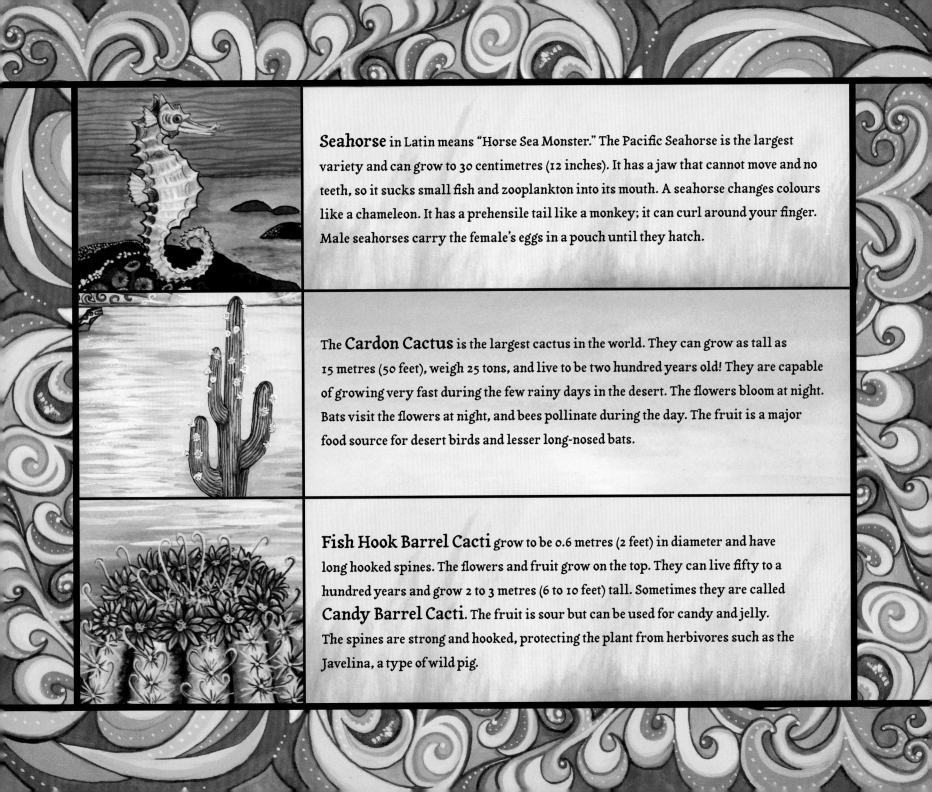

Seahorse in Latin means "Horse Sea Monster." The Pacific Seahorse is the largest variety and can grow to 30 centimetres (12 inches). It has a jaw that cannot move and no teeth, so it sucks small fish and zooplankton into its mouth. A seahorse changes colours like a chameleon. It has a prehensile tail like a monkey; it can curl around your finger. Male seahorses carry the female's eggs in a pouch until they hatch.

The **Cardon Cactus** is the largest cactus in the world. They can grow as tall as 15 metres (50 feet), weigh 25 tons, and live to be two hundred years old! They are capable of growing very fast during the few rainy days in the desert. The flowers bloom at night. Bats visit the flowers at night, and bees pollinate during the day. The fruit is a major food source for desert birds and lesser long-nosed bats.

Fish Hook Barrel Cacti grow to be 0.6 metres (2 feet) in diameter and have long hooked spines. The flowers and fruit grow on the top. They can live fifty to a hundred years and grow 2 to 3 metres (6 to 10 feet) tall. Sometimes they are called **Candy Barrel Cacti**. The fruit is sour but can be used for candy and jelly. The spines are strong and hooked, protecting the plant from herbivores such as the Javelina, a type of wild pig.

The Amazing Grey Whale

Grey whales can grow up to 15 metres (49 feet) long. Adult greys can weigh up to 35 tons! They have a large tail with wide flukes and a notch in the middle. They have rather small flippers. Grey whales have no dorsal fin, but they do have up to nine large bumps on their backs. Grey whales have tough grey skin with spots of white and lighter grey. They also carry patches of white barnacles and patches of yellow and orange parasites.

Calves are almost always born in Baja, Mexico. These babies can be up to 5 metres (17 feet) long and weigh 450 kilograms (1,000 pounds) at birth. They breathe air, and their first breath is taken with their mother lifting the youngster up to the surface of the warm Mexican waters. Calves drink as much as 22 kilograms (50 pounds) of their mother's milk a day, and they gain around the same amount of weight every day! Mother whales stay with them for several months while they learn how to be grey whales.

Adult grey whales have broom-like plates inside their mouth called baleen. They use this in place of teeth. The baleen filters the food from the water. Baleen is made of keratin, the same sort of material our fingernails are made of. They are able to eat hundreds of pounds of food (mostly small fish and zooplankton) every day. This makes the grey whale one of the largest creatures in the sea.

Adult grey whales can grow to be 15 metres (49 feet) long and weigh 40 tons.

Calves are born about 3 metres (17 feet) long and weigh 450 kilograms (1,000 pounds).

Killer Whales can grow to be almost 10 metres (32 feet) long and weigh 6 tons.

Heritage House Publishing Company Ltd.
heritagehouse.ca

CATALOGING INFORMATION AVAILABLE FROM LIBRARY AND ARCHIVES CANADA

978-1-77203-135-5 (cloth) 978-1-77203-163-8 (pbk)
978-1-77203-136-2 (epub) 978-1-77203-137-9 (epdf)

Edited by Lara Kordic
Cover and interior book design by Jacqui Thomas
Cover and interior illustrations by Caroll Simpson

The interior of this book was produced on FSC-certified, acid-free paper,
processed chlorine free and printed with vegetable-based inks.

We acknowledge the financial support of the Government of Canada
through the Canada Book Fund (CBF) and the Canada Council for
the Arts, and the Province of British Columbia through the British
Columbia Arts Council and the Book Publishing Tax Credit.

20 19 18 17 16 1 2 3 4 5

Printed in Canada

AUTHOR'S NOTE

My goal in writing this book is to enhance children's understanding of the
peoples who were here before European contact. I did not set out to retell
the legend of one First Nation. Rather, I wrote my own story of family and
community dynamics, threading into it natural elements common to the North
American West Coast. I also incorporated facts about the amazing grey whale's
migration from Russia through Canadian waters and into Mexican lagoons.
I hope this book will inspire young readers of all ethnicities to further their
knowledge of and respect for First Nations culture, art, and history, and for
the 19,000-kilometre (12,000-mile) migration of the grey whale.

Many sources inspired me. They include Hilary Stewart's *Looking at Indian Art
of the Northwest Coast* (Douglas & McIntyre, 2004) and *Looking at Totem Poles*
(Douglas & McIntyre, 1993); *Indian Myths and Legends from the North Pacific Coast
of America: A Translation of Franz Boas' 1895 Edition of Indianische Sagen von der
Nord-Pacifischen Küste-Amerikas* (Talonbooks, 2006); Rick M. Harbo's *Whelks
to Whales* (Harbour Publishing, 2011); Bill Holm's *Northwest Coast Indian Art:
An Analysis of Form* (University of Washington Press, 1965); Cheryl Shearar's
Understanding Northwest Coast Art: A Guide to Crests, Beings and Symbols
(Douglas & McIntyre, 2000); and Pat Kramer's *Totem Poles* (Heritage House,
2008). I also found useful information at animals.nationalgeographic.com
and seahorseworlds.com/pacific-seahorse.

I dedicate this book to my children, grandchildren, and great-grandchildren.
Let us not place boundaries on our creative thought.